Happy

Mara Bergman
and Simona Sanfilippo

Evans

"This is my dog, Happy," Noah said to Sammy.

"Hello, Happy," said Sammy.

"He likes you," said Noah. "See, he's wagging his tail."

For Nik Graver - MB

First published 2008
Evans Brothers Limited
2A Portman Mansions
Chiltern Street
London W1U 6NR

British Library Cataloguing in Publication Data

Bergman, Mara
    Happy. - (Spirals)
    1. Children's stories
    I. Title
    823.9'2[J]

ISBN-13: 978 0 237 53532 2 (hb)
ISBN-13: 978 0 237 53536 0 (pb)

Printed in China

Editor: Louise John
Design: Robert Walster
Production: Jenny Mulvanny

"Happy's very smart," Noah said.
"What can he do?" asked Sammy.
"He can sit," said Noah. "Happy –
sit, boy!"
Happy sat.

"He can give me his paw," said Noah.
"Happy – paw!"
Happy gave Noah his paw.

"Happy – roll over!" said Noah.

Happy lay on his back, but he didn't roll over.

"He's not so good at that yet," said Noah.

At Sammy's house, Sammy said,
  "Noah, meet my budgie, Sweetie."
  "Hello, Sweetie," said Noah.
  "Sweetie likes you," said Sammy.
  "How can you tell?" asked Noah.
  "She's bobbing up and down," said
Sammy. "That's what she does when she
likes someone."

"Can she do anything else?"
asked Noah.

"Oh, yes," said Sammy. "Sweetie
is very smart. Sweetie – come."

Sweetie hopped up onto
Sammy's wrist.

"Sweetie – walk," said Sammy.
Sweetie walked up Sammy's arm.
"Hello, pretty girl," Sammy said
to her.
"Hello, pretty girl," Sweetie said back
to Sammy.

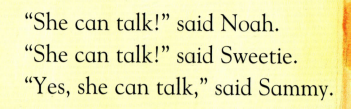

"She can talk!" said Noah.
"She can talk!" said Sweetie.
"Yes, she can talk," said Sammy.

Noah wanted to teach Happy to talk.

"Hello, Happy," Noah said. "How are you, boy?"

Happy just looked at Noah and wagged his tail.

"Don't give up," Sammy said to Noah the next day. "It took me ages to teach Sweetie to talk. You have to keep saying the same words over and over again."

16

After that, every morning, Noah said
to Happy, "Hello, Happy."
   He said it many times, but Happy
just looked at Noah and wagged
his tail.

19

Every afternoon, after school, Noah
said to Happy, "Hello, Happy."

He said it many, many times, but
Happy just looked at Noah and
wagged his tail.

21

Every evening, after dinner, Noah said
to Happy, "Hello, Happy."
He said it many, many, MANY times.
Each time Happy just looked at Noah
and wagged his tail.

"Maybe Happy CAN'T talk," Noah thought at last. "Maybe I'm silly to keep trying."

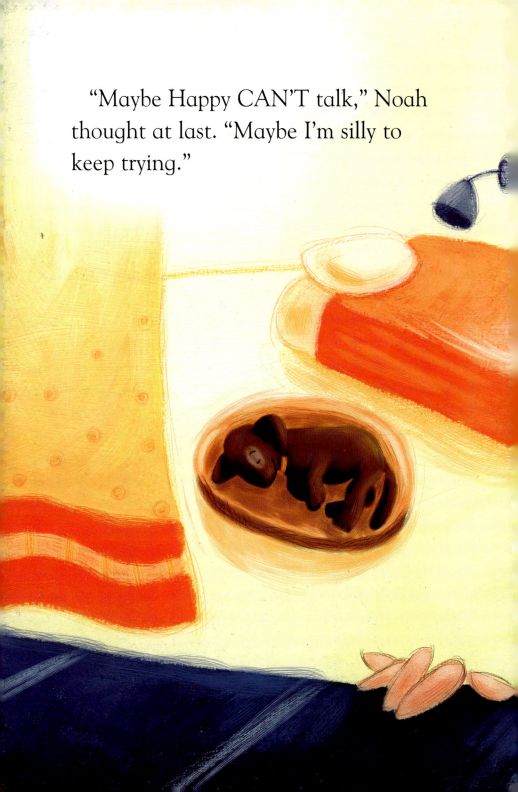

Noah went back to teaching Happy to do the sorts of things that dogs do.

"Happy – beg!"
Happy begged.

"Happy – jump!"
Happy jumped.

"Happy – roll over!" said Noah.

Happy didn't roll over so Noah showed him how to do it.

"Happy – roll over!" said Noah again, and Happy rolled over.

"You are a very clever dog!" said Noah. "Even if you can't talk, you are my clever, clever dog."

Noah gave Happy the biggest hug ever. Happy wagged and wagged his tail.

Brrrrring! Brrrrring!
   The phone was ringing.
   Happy rolled over.
   Brrrrring! Brrrrring!
   Happy jumped up.
   Brrrrring! Brrrrring! Brrrrring!
   The phone kept ringing. This time
Happy picked it up.
   "Hello?" he said. "Happy here."

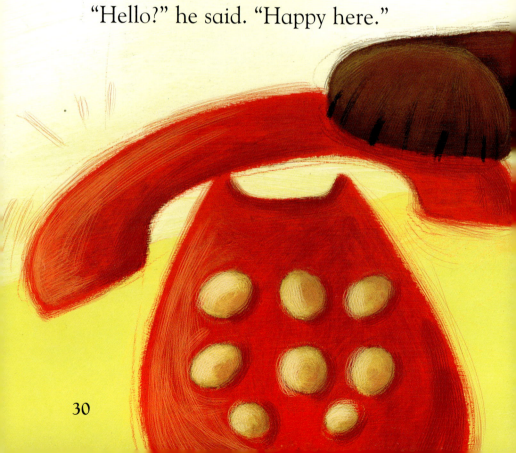

Why not try reading another **Spirals** book?

Megan's Tick Tock Rocket by Andrew Fusek Peters,
Polly Peters and Simona Dimitri
ISBN 978 0237 53348 9 (hb)
ISBN 978 0237 53342 7 (pb)

Growl! by Vivian French and Tim Archbold
ISBN 978 0237 53351 9 (hb)
ISBN 978 0237 53345 8 (pb)

John and the River Monster by Paul Harrison and
Ian Benfold Haywood
ISBN 978 0237 53350 2 (hb)
ISBN 978 0237 53344 1 (pb)

Froggy Went a Hopping by Alan Durant and Sue Mason
ISBN 978 0237 53352 6 (hb)
ISBN 978 0237 53346 5 (pb)

Amy's Slippers by Mary Chapman and Simona Dimitri
ISBN 978 0237 53353 3 (hb)
ISBN 978 0237 53347 2 (pb)

The Flamingo Who Forgot by Alan Durant and Franco Rivolli
ISBN 978 0237 53349 6 (hb)
ISBN 978 0237 53343 4 (pb)

Glub! by Penny Little and Sue Mason
ISBN 978 0237 53462 2 (hb)
ISBN 978 0237 53461 5 (pb)

The Grumpy Queen by Valerie Wilding and Simona Sanfilippo
ISBN 978 0237 53460 8 (hb)
ISBN 978 0237 53459 2 (pb)

Happy by Mara Bergman and Simona Sanfilippo
ISBN 978 0237 53532 2 (hb)
ISBN 978 0237 53536 0 (pb)

Sink or Swim by Dereen Taylor and Marijke van Veldhoven
ISBN 978 0237 53531 5 (hb)
ISBN 978 0237 53535 3 (pb)

Sophie's Timepiece by Mary Chapman and Nigel Baines
ISBN 978 0237 53530 8 (hb)
ISBN 978 0237 53534 6 (pb)